This book belongs to

Published by Big Idea Entertainment, 320 Billingsly Court, Suite 30, Franklin, TN 37067

ISBN: 978-1-60587-226-1

Printed in China

First Big Idea Printing, February 2011

VeggieTales®

Good Knight, Duke

A Lesson in
Being Nice

by Ronald Kidd

Illustrated by
Tod Carter and
Joe Spadaford

A long time ago, in the Kingdom of Scone, there lived a duke named . . . well . . . Duke. He was tall and green and handsome.

(In fact, he was probably a lot like you, if you're a cucumber.)

The Duke of Scone lived in a castle at the top of the hill. Right down the road lived his best friend Petunia and her mother-in-law, Nona. Nona complained a lot, but not Petunia. She was known as the sweetest person in the kingdom. She loved to bake cookies, cakes, and pies. All of them were sweet, but Petunia was sweeter.

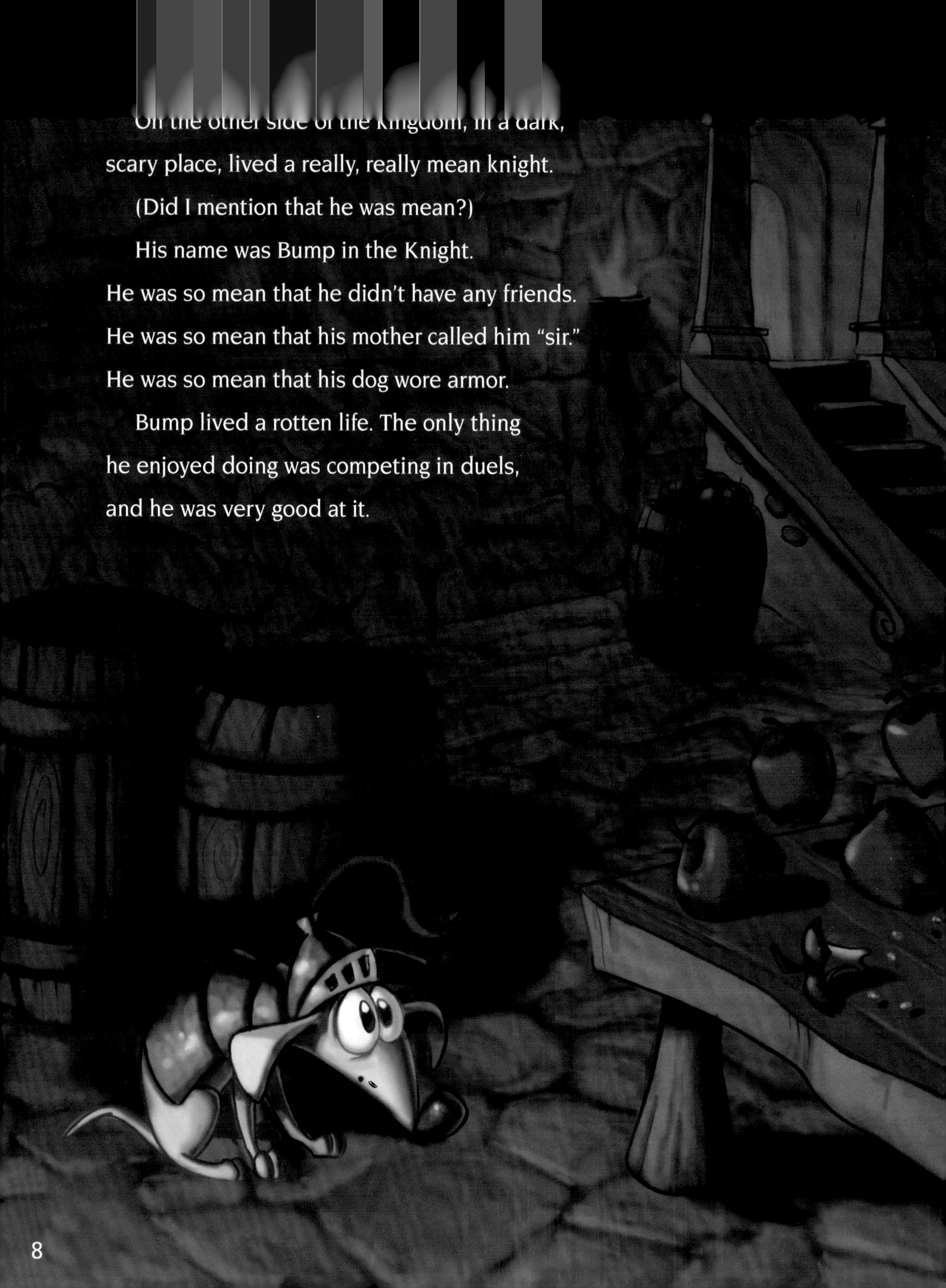

On the other side of the kingdom, in a dark, scary place, lived a really, really mean knight.

(Did I mention that he was mean?)

His name was Bump in the Knight. He was so mean that he didn't have any friends. He was so mean that his mother called him "sir." He was so mean that his dog wore armor.

Bump lived a rotten life. The only thing he enjoyed doing was competing in duels, and he was very good at it.

Now, Duke loved to throw parties. He and the Knights of the Square Table would water-ski in the moat and play croquet on the lawn. Petunia would serve cookies. Nona would complain.

"I hate water," Nona would often say. "It's too wet."

One day while riding by Duke's castle, Bump saw something that made him angry. People at Duke's party were laughing. People were playing. People were having fun.

Gasp!

Bump never had fun, and he didn't want anybody else to either. So he yelled, "Duke, I challenge you to a duel. I'll stop these silly parties once and for all."

(See? I told you he was mean.)

"There will be three events in the duel: pie jousting, doughnut tossing, and pastry pulling," Bump said.

Duke knew he had to face Bump. "I accept the challenge," Duke said nervously.

Word spread quickly, the people immediately began preparations and made signs to announce the duel. The winner would receive the most prized trophy of all—the Golden Spatula of Scone! And the loser would have to stop throwing loud, happy parties.

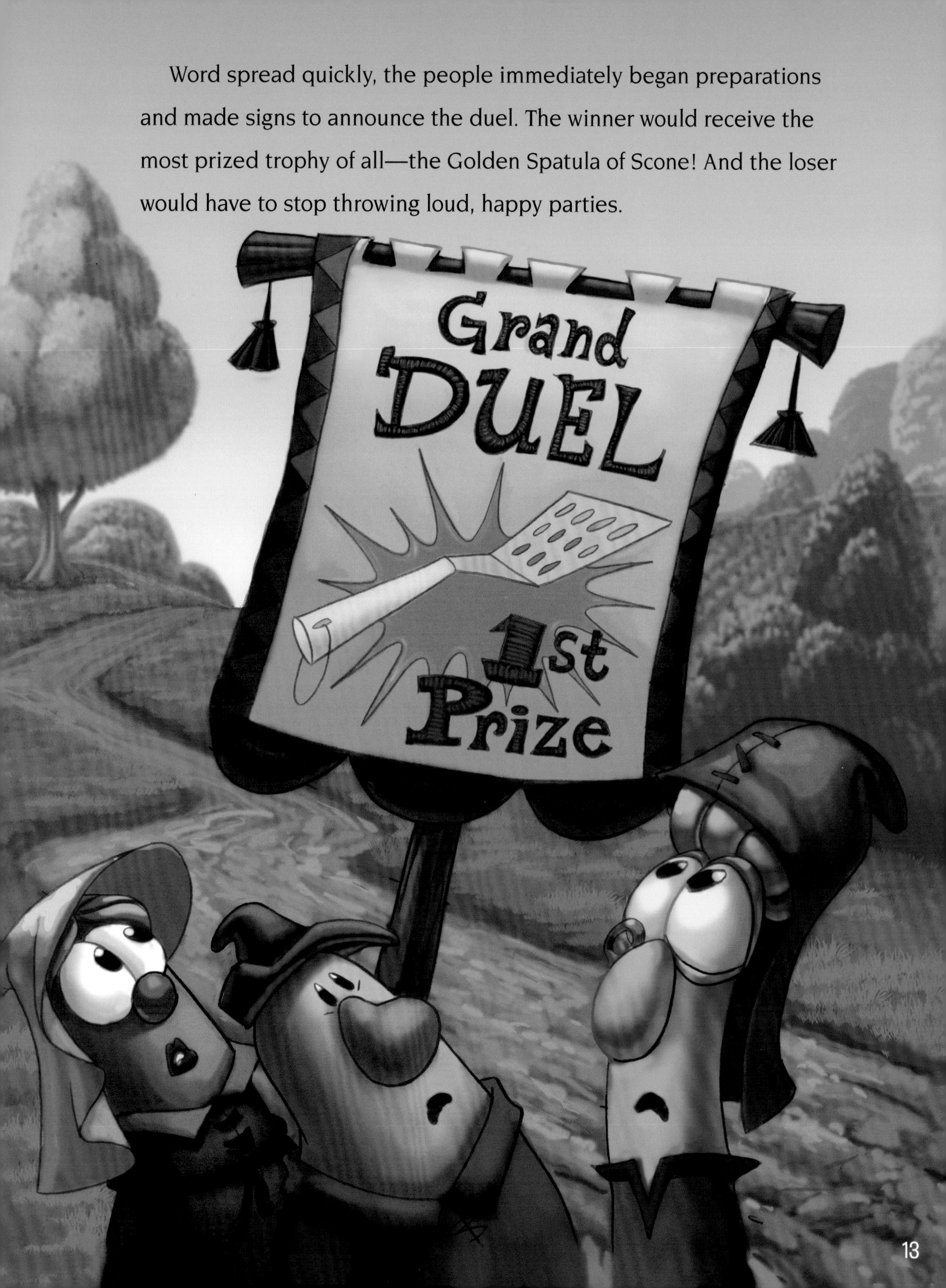

Despite his nervousness, Duke started to train, coached by the Knights of the Square Table and their leader, Otis the Elevated.

Otis watched Duke train and shook his head. "You call that pie jousting?"

But Duke was determined, and he soon improved his jousting, tossing, and pulling. He also got in a little water-skiing.

DUEL
TODAY

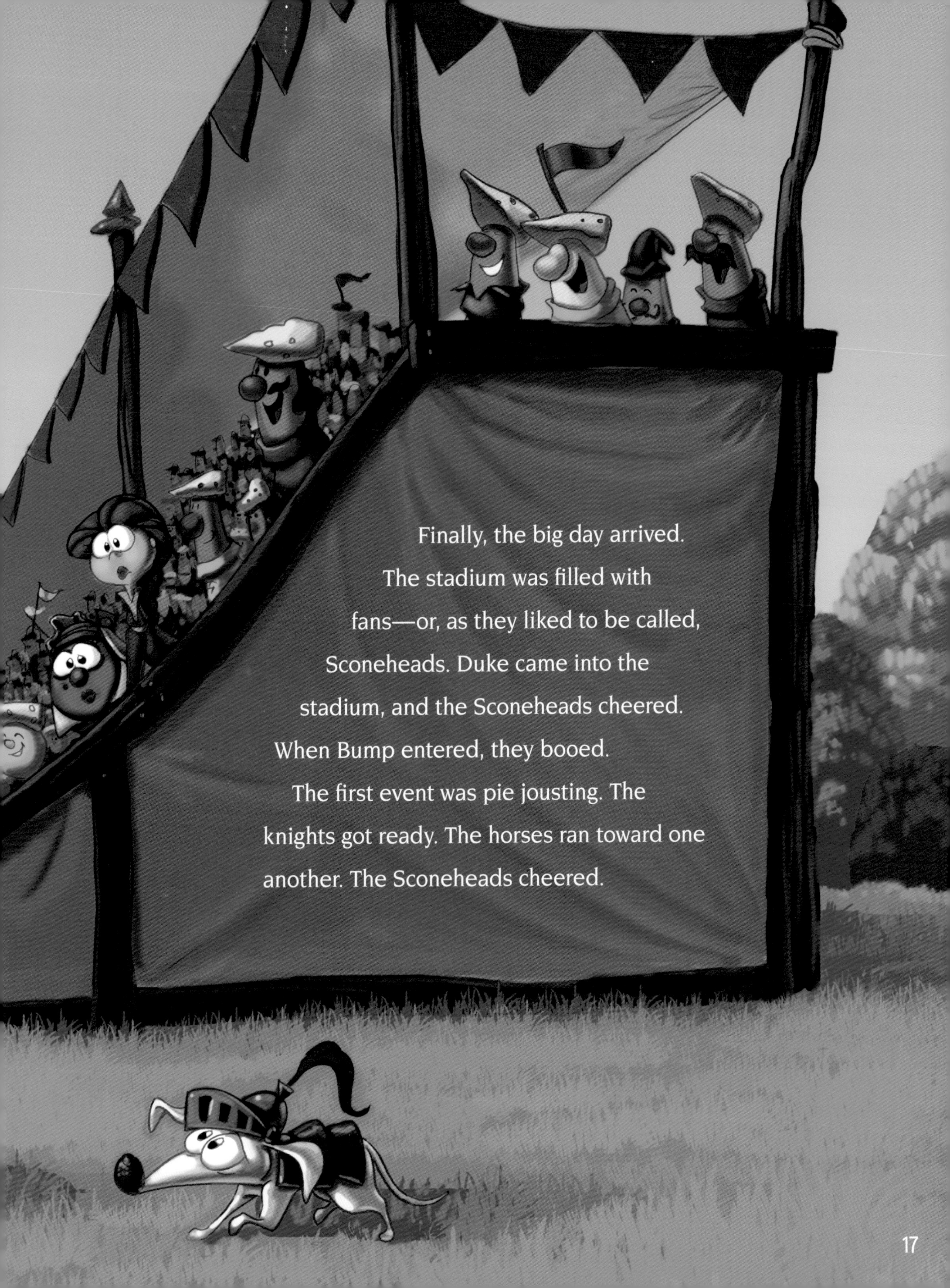

Finally, the big day arrived. The stadium was filled with fans—or, as they liked to be called, Sconeheads. Duke came into the stadium, and the Sconeheads cheered. When Bump entered, they booed.

The first event was pie jousting. The knights got ready. The horses ran toward one another. The Sconeheads cheered.

Duke turned to wave to his loyal fans—
big mistake!
WHAM!

The next thing Duke knew, he was lying flat on his back. The bad news was that he had lost the event. The good news was that he had pie on his face. It was banana cream—***Yum!***

Bump looked down at Duke and laughed. "Score: one to nothing!" Bump bragged.

Next was donut tossing. Otis made the donuts for this event himself. "You could break your tooth on these babies!" Otis laughed.

Besides being hard, the donuts were so heavy that Duke could barely lift them.

Meanwhile, Bump tossed them around like pebbles. In fact, he tossed one so hard, it *accidentally* missed its target and hit Duke right in the forehead.

(Guess who won the event?)

Bump laughed. "Score: two for **Bump** in the Knight, zero for Bump in the *head!*"

There was just one event left—pastry pulling. Duke was determined to win. But he was tired and hungry, and he had a pounding headache.

In the stands, Nona turned to Petunia to complain, but Petunia had left. Seeing that Duke was in trouble, she had decided to help.

(How, you ask?)

The way she always helped—by baking. Petunia had gone home, baked a Peanut Butter and Tuna Pot Pie, hurried back to the stadium, and handed Duke the pie.

As Duke ate, he noticed Bump sitting by himself. Bump looked mean, as usual. But he also looked sad and lonely.

Duke took the pie and sat down next to Bump. "Would you like some?" asked Duke.

Bump stared at him. Then he did an amazing thing—he started to cry. "That's the nicest thing anybody ever said to me," he blubbered. "You're a good knight, Duke."

Duke said, "Maybe so, but you're a strong knight."

Bump shook his head. "I'm not strong. You're the one who's strong, because you're nice. From now on," said Bump, "I'm going to be strong, just like you."

Duke and Bump finished the pot pie, then they went out and pulled pastry. Bump won, of course, and was awarded the Golden Spatula.

Bump could have been mean about winning. But instead, he invited everyone to a party at Duke's castle.

Because of Duke, Bump in the Knight had learned how to be strong—not by being mean, but by being nice.

Otis, who was watching, leaned over to Nona. "You know, I always liked that Bump in the Knight."

Nona, who was eating a piece of pie, tried to come up with a complaint. But a funny thing happened—she couldn't think of a single one.

Make sure that nobody pays back one wrong act with another.
Always try to be kind to each other and to everyone else.
1 Thessalonians 5:15

Duke turned to wave to his loyal fans—
big mistake!
WHAM!

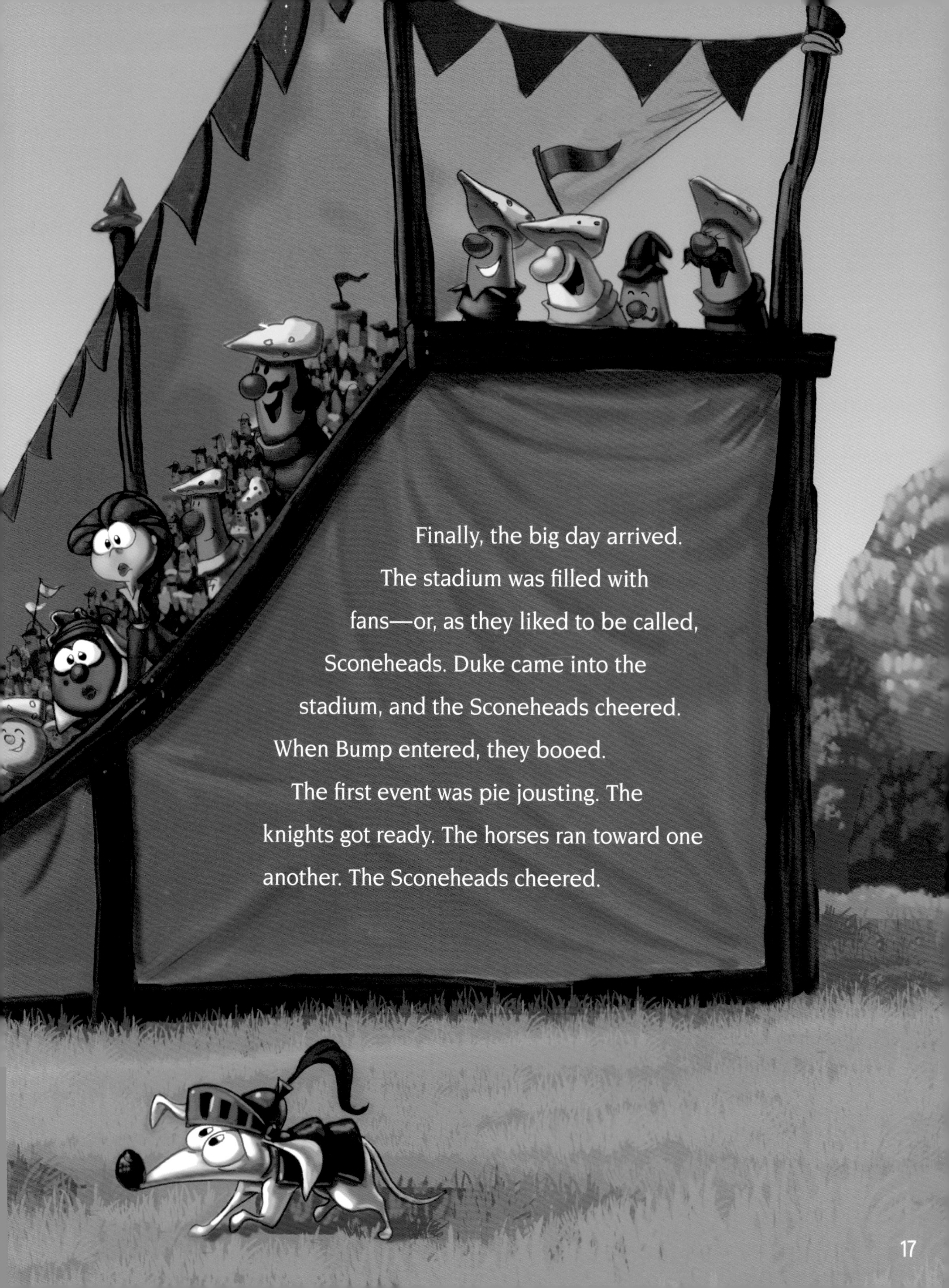

Finally, the big day arrived. The stadium was filled with fans—or, as they liked to be called, Sconeheads. Duke came into the stadium, and the Sconeheads cheered. When Bump entered, they booed.

The first event was pie jousting. The knights got ready. The horses ran toward one another. The Sconeheads cheered.